Acting Edition

M000074133

Rodgers & Hammerstein's Cinderella

Music by
Richard Rodgers

Lyrics by
Oscar Hammerstein II

Orchestrations by
Robert Russell Bennett

CONCORD
THEATRICALS

FOR PRODUCTION INQUIRIES

UNITED STATES AND CANADA
info@concordtheatricals.com
1-866-979-0447

UNITED KINGDOM AND EUROPE
licensing@concordtheatricals.co.uk
020-7054-7298

Each title is subject to availability from Concord Theatricals Corp.,
depending upon country of performance. Please be aware that
CINDERELLA may not be licensed by Concord Theatricals Corp. in
your territory. Professional and amateur producers should contact the
nearest Concord Theatricals Corp. office or licensing partner to verify
availability.

THIRD-PARTY MATERIALS USE NOTE

IMPORTANT BILLING AND CREDIT REQUIREMENTS

CINDERELLA was originally presented by CBS-Television on March 31, 1957. The production was produced by Richard Lewine and directed by Ralph Nelson, with choreography by Jonathan Lucas, settings and costumes by William and Jean Eckart, technical direction by Lou Tedesco, musical direction by Alfredo Antonini, orchestrations by Robert Russell Bennett, set decoration by Gene Callahan, lighting direction by Robert Barry, and associate direction by Rowland Vance. The stage manager was Joseph Papp. The cast was as follows:

CINDERELLA . . . . .Julie Andrews

KING. . . . . .Howard Lindsay

QUEEN. . . . . Dorothy Stickney

STEPMOTHER. . . . . Ilka Chase

PORTIA. . . . . Kaye Ballard

JOY . . . . .Alice Ghostley

PRINCE CHARMING. . . . . Jon Cypher

FAIRY GODMOTHER. . . . . .Edith Adams

TOWN CRIER . . . . Robert Penn

CAPTAIN OF THE GUARD . . . . Alec Clarke

CHEF. . . . . .Iggie Wolfington

STEWARD. . . . . .George Hall

COURT TAILOR . . . . David F. Perkins

TOWNSPEOPLE. . . . . Eleanor Pheips, Martha Greenhouse,
Jerome Collamore, Julius J. Bloom,
Jacquelyn Paige, John Call

CHILDREN . . . . Kathy Kelly, Karen Lock, Leland Mayforth,
Johnny Towsen, Karen Waters

SINGERS & DANCERS . . . . Charles Aschmann, Herb Banke,
Donald Barton, Hank Brunjes, Robert Burland,
Jean Caples, Jean Coates, Sally Crane,
Richard Crowley, William Damian, Grace Dorian,
Debbie Douglas, Jose Falcion, Pat Finch,
Marvin Goodis, Gloria Hamilton, Dorothy Hill,
Stuart Hodes, Diana Hunter, Joseph Layton,
Margot Moser, Giselle Orkin, Hazel Patterson,
Alex Polermo, Earl Rogers, John Smolko,
Tao Strong, Jayne Turner

CHARACTERS

CINDERELLA

PRINCE

KING

QUEEN

STEPMOTHER

PORTIA

JOY

GODMOTHER

HERALD

CHEF

STEWARD

COACHMAN

FOOTMAN

GUARDS

MINISTER

GUESTS AT THE BALL

TOWNSPEOPLE

CHILDREN

INCLUSION STATEMENT

In this show, the race of the characters is not pivotal to the plot. We encourage you to consider diversity and inclusion in your casting choices.

ADDITIONAL SONG

In Act I, Scene Three, an additional song, Music No. 07B "Loneliness of Evening," sung by Prince Charming, can be added immediately following Music No. 07A "Your Majesties (Dance)." Please contact Concord Theatricals to license the music for this song.

SYNOPSIS OF SCENES

ACT I

Scene One: The Public Square
Scene Two: Cinderella's House
Scene Three: The Royal Dressing Room
Scene Four: Cinderella's House

ACT II

Scene One: Outside the Palace
Scene Two: The Palace Ballroom
Scene Three: The Palace Garden
Scene Four: The Palace Ballroom
Scene Five: The Palace Garden

ACT III

Scene One: Cinderella's House
Scene Two: The Royal Dressing Room
Scene Three: The Public Square
Scene Four: Cinderella's House
Scene Five: The Palace Garden

MUSICAL NUMBERS

ACT I

"The Prince Is Giving A Ball"....................Herald, Townspeople

"In My Own Little Corner".............................. Cinderella

"Your Majesties"................................... Chef, Steward,
King, Queen

"Your Majesties (Dance)" ....Chefs, Stewards,
King, Queen

"Boys And Girls Like You And Me"....................King & Queen

"In My Own Little Corner (Reprise) into Fol-De-Rol" ..... Cinderella &
Godmother

"Impossible" .... Cinderella & Godmother

"It's Possible"............................. Cinderella & Godmother

ACT II

"Ten Minutes Ago"............................Cinderella & Prince

"Stepsisters' Lament"................................Joy & Portia

"Waltz For A Ball" .... Chorus

"Do I Love You Because You're Beautiful?".........Cinderella & Prince

ACT III

"When You're Driving Through The Moonlight"............Cinderella,
Stepmother,
Joy, Portia

"A Lovely Night" ....Cinderella,
Stepmother,
Joy, Portia

"A Lovely Night (Coda)" .... Cinderella

"Do I Love You Because You're Beautiful? (Reprise)"... Queen & Prince

"Finale: The Wedding" .... Company

start stage left w/ zack

ACT I

[MUSIC NO. 01 "OVERTURE"]

Scene One

[MUSIC NO. 02 "CURTAIN MUSIC ACT I"]

(The public square. At rise, a busy afternoon is interrupted by a trumpet fanfare. Groups of **TOWNSPEOPLE** *look up from their chores and their shopping,* **PEDESTRIANS** *stop in their tracks, and* **CHILDREN** *pour out of houses to see what is happening. The* **HERALD** *is standing on a platform stage center between two red-faced* **TRUMPETERS**, *the source of the fanfare. His stiff-backed formality barely conceals his excitement at his own news.)*

(Optional: The **GODMOTHER** *appears in front of the curtain and, with a wave of her wand, brings the curtain up. Then, with successive waves, she awakens the town from a frozen tableau. Once she has brought the town to life, she exits.)*

[MUSIC NO. 03 "THE PRINCE IS GIVING A BALL"]

HERALD.
    THE PRINCE IS GIVING A BALL!   *Kneel stage right*
TOWNSPEOPLE. *(Surprised and delighted with the news.)*
    THE PRINCE IS GIVING A BALL!
    THE PRINCE IS GIVING A BALL!

1

HERALD. *(Reading from a scroll, he tries to deliver the whole message without taking a breath.)*

HIS ROYAL HIGHNESS, CHRISTOPHER RUPERT
WINDEMERE VLADIMIR KARL ALEXANDER
FRANCOIS REGINALD LAUNCELOT HERMAN –

LITTLE BOY.

HERMAN?

HERALD.

– HERMAN GREGORY JAMES

(Breathes.)

IS GIVING A BALL!

TOWNSPEOPLE.

THE PRINCE IS GIVING A BALL!
THE PRINCE IS GIVING A BALL!

> *(The* **CROWD** *scatters to spread the news. From different areas of the stage, the following lines are sung by characters in distinct groups: a family [***FATHER**,* **MOTHER**, *and* **DAUGHTER**]*; a group of* **GIRLS***; a second group of* **GIRLS***.)*

FATHER.

OUR DAUGHTER'S LOOKING DREAMY-EYED.

MOTHER. *(Providing the obvious explanation.)*

THE PRINCE IS GIVING A BALL.

DAUGHTER. *(Dreamy-eyed.)*

THEY SAY HE WANTS TO FIND A BRIDE;
HE MAY FIND ONE AT THE BALL.

FIRST GIRL. *(To* **SECOND GIRL**.*)*

IF ONLY HE'D PROPOSE TO ME.

SECOND GIRL. *(To* **THIRD GIRL**.*)*

I PRAY THAT HE'LL PROPOSE TO ME.

THIRD GIRL. *(To herself.)*

WHY *SHOULDN'T* HE PROPOSE TO ME?

WOMAN.

I WISH I HADN'T MARRIED SAM.
(To **DAUGHTER**.*)* PULL IN YOUR LITTLE DIAPHRAGM.

[Handwritten margin note: Stage left w/ fam & dance]

OLDEST SISTER. *(Smugly.)*

I'LL WEAR A GOWN OF SATIN JADE.

YOUNGER SISTER.

AND ME, I'M IN A PINK BROCADE.

KID SISTER. *(Putting her inconsolable chin on her two little fists.)*

AND ME, I'M IN THE SECOND GRADE!

TOWNSPEOPLE.

THE PRINCE IS GIVING A BALL!

THE PRINCE IS GIVING A BALL!

HERALD.

HIS ROYAL HIGHNESS, CHRISTOPHER RUPERT,

SON OF HER MAJESTY, QUEEN CONSTANTINA

CHARLOTTE ERMINTRUDE, GWINYVERE MAISIE –

LITTLE BOY. *(Same one as before.)*

MAISIE?

HERALD.

– MAISIE MARGUERITE ANNE IS GIVING A BALL!

TOWNSPEOPLE.

THE PRINCE IS GIVING A BALL!

THE PRINCE IS GIVING A BALL!

SLOPPY GIRL.

I WISH I DIDN'T LIKE TO EAT.

BAD GIRL. *(À la Mae West.)*

I WISH I WERE DEMURE AND SWEET.

STUDIOUS GIRL. *(With spectacles.)*

I WISH I WERE A BOLDER GIRL.

GRANDMA.

I WISH I WERE A YOUNGER GIRL.

KID SISTER. *(Same one as before.)*

I WISH I WERE AN OLDER GIRL!

TOWNSPEOPLE.

THE PRINCE IS GIVING A BALL!

THE PRINCE IS GIVING A BALL!

HERALD.

HIS ROYAL HIGHNESS, CHRISTOPHER RUPERT,

SON OF HIS MAJESTY, KING MAXIMILLIAN
GODFREY LADISLAUS LEOPOLD SIDNEY –

TOWNSPEOPLE.
SIDNEY?   *pop up*

HERALD.
– SIDNEY! FREDERICK JOHN
IS GIVING A BALL.   *Back to*
                                     stor

TOWNSPEOPLE.
THE PRINCE IS GIVING A BALL!
THE PRINCE IS GIVING A BALL!
THE PRINCE IS GIVING A BALL!

(The song ends with everyone frozen in a tableau.)

[MUSIC NO. 04 "CINDERELLA MARCH"]

*(The **STEPMOTHER**, **JOY**, and **PORTIA** enter as the freeze is broken. They walk in time to the music, and behind them the town comes to life in pantomime.)*

*(The three are dressed magnificently and walk with an obvious sense of their own importance. The **STEPMOTHER** is rather imperious, as befits a proper stepmother, but there is no happy light in **JOY** and no suggestion of intelligence in **PORTIA**. In fact the two stepsisters have been named in direct opposition to their true demeanor, for we will never see a true smile cross **JOY**'s face, and it is obvious **PORTIA** isn't bright enough to be a great lawyer like her namesake.)*

*(**TOWNSPEOPLE** pass them on the street and greet them and get nothing more than a rather sour formal bow in return. Strange looks come over the faces of the **TOWNSPEOPLE**, and as the trio passes through the town square we see behind them the object of the strange looks: a **YOUNG GIRL** invisible behind a prodigious pile of packages and parcels.)*

(*As the* **STEPMOTHER**, **PORTIA**, *and* **JOY** *cross out of the picture, the parcels teeter ominously, and the* **GIRL** *halts, gaining control of them just in the nick of time. As she pauses to catch her breath and re-balance her load, we see her face for the first time, peeking through the wall of packages. It is* **CINDERELLA**.)

STEPMOTHER. (*Re-enters impatiently.*) Cinderella! Come along home now. You're cluttering up the street!

(*The* **STEPMOTHER** *exits, and* **CINDERELLA** *picks up her packages and follows. As she does, the town disappears, and Cinderella's house appears.*)

Scene Two

(While the "Cinderella March" continues, **JOY**, **PORTIA**, *and the* **STEPMOTHER** *enter the house.* **CINDERELLA** *enters with great difficulty, her pile of packages too tall, too wide, and too big for the doorway to the modest house. But somehow she makes it.)*

(As soon as **CINDERELLA** *enters, the family starts ordering her about. During the next sequence,* **CINDERELLA** *somehow satisfies every demand without making a mistake or missing a beat. She is a very efficient girl who always completes everything demanded of her. By the end she will have done everything asked of her and successfully served tea as well. The music continues as underscoring until she shuts the window for the final time.)*

STEPMOTHER. Cinderella, the door.

> *(***CINDERELLA*** closes the door.)*

JOY. Cinderella, close the window.

> *(***CINDERELLA*** closes it, but it springs back open.)*

PORTIA. *(Expecting* **CINDERELLA** *to pull it out.)* Cinderella, my chair.

> *(***CINDERELLA*** pulls out her chair for her.)*

STEPMOTHER. Cinderella, close the window.

> *(***CINDERELLA*** closes it, but it springs back open.)*

JOY. Cinderella, my chair.

> *(***CINDERELLA*** comes toward her.)*

PORTIA. Cinderella, close the window.

> *(***CINDERELLA*** closes it, but it springs back open.)*

JOY. Cinderella, my chair!

(**CINDERELLA** *pulls out her chair for her.*)

STEPMOTHER. Cinderella, make some tea, honey.

PORTIA. Cinderella, iron my dress. I'll need it.

STEPMOTHER. Cinderella, lay out my new gown for this evening.

JOY. Cinderella, wash my gloves for tomorrow.

PORTIA. Cinderella, it's freezing!

(**CINDERELLA** *leaves the fireplace, where she is making tea, to close the window. It springs back open.*)

STEPMOTHER. Cinderella, poke the fire.

(**CINDERELLA** *returns to the fireplace.*)

JOY. Cinderella, close the window.

(**CINDERELLA** *closes the window. It springs open.*)

PORTIA. Really, Cinderella

STEPMOTHER. Cinderella, really.

JOY. It's freezing!

(**CINDERELLA** *closes the window. It opens.*)

PORTIA. Close the window.

(**CINDERELLA** *gives her a cup of tea.*)

JOY. Close the window.

(**CINDERELLA** *gives her a cup of tea.*)

STEPMOTHER. Close the window, Cinderella!

(**CINDERELLA** *gives her a cup of tea and closes the window firmly and finally.*)

(*Music stops.*)

Now, my daughters, I want to talk to you.

(**CINDERELLA** *approaches with a smile.*)

Well, not you – I want to talk to my *own* daughters.

(**CINDERELLA**, *still trying to smile, goes meekly to her corner by the fireplace.* **JOY** *and* **PORTIA** *smugly gather around their* **MOTHER**.)

JOY. That girl always wants to sit down. No wonder she never gets anything done.

STEPMOTHER. Now, Joy...

JOY. Yes ma'am.

STEPMOTHER. ...and Portia...

PORTIA. Yes, ma'am.

STEPMOTHER. As you well know, my little moppets, this *may* be the most important year of your lives. The Prince has returned from his studies abroad, and this ball that's being given in his honor is for one purpose only.

PORTIA. They want him to choose a bride.

(She laughs her goofy laugh.)

STEPMOTHER. Every girl in the kingdom wants to marry the Prince. Including you, Portia.

PORTIA. Uh-huh.

STEPMOTHER. And you, Joy.

JOY. *(Sourly.)* Uh-huh.

STEPMOTHER. On our shopping tour today I bought you the most beautiful materials and all the frills and froufrou my purse could afford. *(Her voice hardens.)* So whether or not you marry the Prince, you'll both have to marry somebody this year.

PORTIA. *(Snapping into frightened obedience.)* Yes, ma'am.

JOY. Yes, ma'am.

STEPMOTHER. *(Her voice softening again.)* Now there's one thing you must remember. When you want to marry a man, you can't rely on your beauty alone. Now, Portia – you are named for a great lawyer.

PORTIA. Uh-huh.

STEPMOTHER. I want you to show off your intellect as well as your beauty. Do you understand?

PORTIA. Naturally.

STEPMOTHER. And Joy, I want you to live up to your name. I want you to be vivacious and alert as well as beautiful.

JOY. Uh-huh.

STEPMOTHER. That does not mean, however, that I want you to neglect your appearance. Our family has always been noted for its fascinating women. So now let's all go upstairs and get our beauty sleep. I'm exhausted from all that shopping. Tomorrow I'm going to have to get a massage. That's the only thing that does me any good – a good pounding. That's what your father used to say.

PORTIA. *(Following her to the stairs.)* I'm all tired out, too, Ma, going from store to store the way we did.

> (**JOY** *and* **PORTIA** *climb the stairs, arguing with each other.)*

JOY. *You're* tired?

PORTIA. Yes, *I'm* tired.

JOY. I suppose you think you're the only one that's tired!

PORTIA. Well, who bought the most?

JOY. That has nothing to do with it!

PORTIA. That has everything to do with it!

STEPMOTHER. Go to bed, both of you!

PORTIA. *(To* **JOY** *as they exit.)* Leave me alone... You're always picking on me... Ma!

STEPMOTHER. That's right, don't raise your voices.

> *(She is at the bottom of the stairs and turns to see* **CINDERELLA** *standing there expectantly.)*

Well, you – don't stand there gaping at me. Tidy up those tea things.

CINDERELLA. Yes ma'am.

> *(The* **STEPMOTHER** *turns on her heel and goes upstairs.* **CINDERELLA** *brings a dishpan with water and a rag to the table and washes the tea things.)*

CINDERELLA. *(Happily.)* I wonder why they're so tired, looking at all those beautiful things and buying so many of them! I was too excited to be tired.

> *(She looks around the room.)*

[MUSIC NO. 05 "IN MY OWN LITTLE CORNER"]

Oh, I love this room – when they've all gone out and there's nobody here but me.

> *(Drying a teacup, she dances around the room happily.)*

STEPMOTHER. *(Offstage.)* Cinderella!

CINDERELLA. *(Stopping, frightened.)* Yes, ma'am?

STEPMOTHER. Stop jumping around down there like an elephant! We can't sleep for the racket!

CINDERELLA. Yes, ma'am.

> *(She crosses past the table to her little chair in the corner by the fireplace. She is penitent, not angry.)*

I was just going to sit down, anyway. *(Brightening.)* I love sitting down right here.

> *(The lights change as she muses. The music becomes gentler, and she sings.)*

I'M AS MILD AND AS MEEK AS A MOUSE,
WHEN I HEAR A COMMAND I OBEY.
BUT I KNOW OF A SPOT IN MY HOUSE
WHERE NO ONE CAN STAND IN MY WAY.

IN MY OWN LITTLE CORNER,
IN MY OWN LITTLE CHAIR,
I CAN BE WHATEVER I WANT TO BE.
ON THE WING OF MY FANCY
I CAN FLY ANYWHERE
AND THE WORLD WILL OPEN ITS ARMS TO ME.
I'M A YOUNG NORWEGIAN PRINCE OR A MILK MAID,
I'M THE GREATEST PRIMA DONNA IN MILAN,
I'M AN HEIRESS WHO HAS ALWAYS HAD HER SILK MADE

BY HER OWN FLOCK OF SILKWORMS IN JAPAN!
I'M A GIRL MEN GO MAD FOR,
LOVE'S A GAME I CAN PLAY
WITH A COOL AND CONFIDENT KIND OF AIR,
JUST AS LONG AS I STAY
IN MY OWN LITTLE CORNER,
ALL ALONE
IN MY OWN
LITTLE CHAIR

(She dances around a bit.)

I CAN BE WHATEVER I WANT TO BE.
I'M A THIEF IN CALCUTTA,
I'M A QUEEN IN PERU,
I'M A MERMAID DANCING UPON THE SEA.
I'M A HUNTRESS ON AN AFRICAN SAFARI –
(IT'S A DANGEROUS TYPE OF SPORT AND YET IT'S FUN.)
IN THE NIGHT I SALLY FORTH TO SEEK MY QUARRY
AND I FIND I FORGOT TO BRING MY GUN!
I AM LOST IN THE JUNGLE
ALL ALONE AND UNARMED
WHEN I MEET A LIONESS IN HER LAIR!
THEN I'M GLAD TO BE BACK IN MY OWN LITTLE CORNER,
ALL ALONE
IN MY OWN
LITTLE CHAIR.

(Blackout.)

Scene Three

[MUSIC NO. 06 "CHANGE OF SCENE (THE PRINCE IS GIVING A BALL)"]

(In the blackout, the house unit is moved upstage, the fireplace unit is brought downstage and spun around, the drop descends, and we are in the royal dressing room.)

(The QUEEN *sits at a chair, sewing a button on the king's trousers. The* KING, *clad only in his shirt and underwear, strides angrily across the room to bang the window shut and drown out the voices from the street. They both wear their crowns.)*

Thumbs up backstage have

VOICES. *(Offstage.)*

THE PRINCE IS GIVING A BALL! THE PRINCE IS GIVING A BALL!

KING. *(Derisively imitating the crowd.)* The Prince is giving a ball!

(Pointing an accusing finger at his wife.)

You got us into this!

QUEEN. *(Happily.)* We had to do something to celebrate the twenty-first birthday of our son –

(Bursting into song.)

– HIS ROYAL HIGHNESS, CHRISTOPHER RUPERT...

KING. Maisie...

QUEEN.

...WINDEMERE VLADIMIR...

KING. Maisie...MAISIE!

(He has shouted her down.)

I know all his names. I'm his father.

QUEEN. A fine father you are!

(She hands him his trousers.)

KING. *(Starting to put them on.)* What do you mean, *(Imitating her.)* "A fine father you are"?

QUEEN. I mean you never worry about him.

KING. *(A little breathless from the physical effort of balancing on one leg.)* Why should I...worry about him?

QUEEN. Because he isn't happy!

KING. How do you know?

> *(He is now struggling to make his trousers meet at the waistline – obviously a futile project.)*

QUEEN. He doesn't seem to have any interest in anything – or anyone.

KING. *(Not a man to face unpleasant facts.)* Oh, he's happy all right.

QUEEN. *(As if this clinches the argument.)* If he's happy, why doesn't he get married?

KING. *(Still trying to make the top button approach the top buttonhole.)* If he's happy why...should he...get married?

> *(He gives up the struggle. The two top buttons have to stay unbuttoned. He sits down, defeated.)*

QUEEN. Look at your pants!

KING. How could I have gained so much weight in five years?

QUEEN. Because that's all you've *done* for five years – gained weight! You haven't worn a court costume because we haven't given a ball for five years. You've done nothing to give your subjects any fun – not a festival! Not a fair! Not a pageant! You've done nothing to make your people love you!

KING. *(Smiling smugly.)* Ah, but they do anyway.

> *(The **QUEEN** gives him a cool, silent glance.)*

Don't they?

> *(The **QUEEN** shakes her head slowly and emphatically.)*

KING. Oh.

QUEEN. The royal tailor will have to make you another suit.

KING. That'll cost money.

QUEEN. Don't start to worry about what you're going to pay the tailor. Wait until you see what this ball is going to cost.

KING. Maisie, this is no time to splurge. The exchequer is very low and I can't afford...

QUEEN. I have the chef and the steward outside waiting to report their plans for the dinner.

KING. The dinner!

QUEEN. Certainly. You can't give a ball without a dinner.

> *(She has gone to the door and opened it.)*

Come in, gentlemen.

KING. *(In an irritated whisper.)* Don't have them in here!

> *(He grabs his dressing gown and holds it across his non-meeting trousers as the* **CHEF** *and the* **STEWARD** *enter.)*

[MUSIC NO. 07 "YOUR MAJESTIES"]

CHEF. *(Bowing.)*
> YOUR MAJESTIES.

STEWARD. *(Bowing.)*
> YOUR MAJESTIES.

CHEF. *(Handing the* **QUEEN** *a long list, which she unrolls.)*
> A LIST OF THE BARE NECESSITIES.

KING. *(In an irritated whisper.)*
> A LIST OF THE BARE NECESSITIES FOR WHAT?

QUEEN.
> FOR SEVENTEEN HUNDRED GUESTS!

KING.
> THAT SEEMS A LOT.
> Don't have any king crab.

CHEF. Very well, Your Majesty.

KING. I hate to see that written on a menu – "king crab" – seems like a comment on my disposition.

(The **QUEEN** *glares at him and then starts to read from the list.)*

QUEEN.

A THOUSAND BABY LOBSTERS FOR THE SALAD.

KING. Wow!

QUEEN.

AND FIVE HUNDRED PHEASANT FOR THE PIE.

KING. Ai-yai!

QUEEN.

A THOUSAND POUNDS OF CAVIAR.

KING.

A THOUSAND!

QUEEN. Hush.

KING.

IT'S MORE THAN THE STURGEON CAN SUPPLY!

CHEF.

I TOLD THE STEWARD TO GET US
FORTY ACRES OF LETTUCE
AND SIX HUNDRED SUCKLING PIGS FOR ROASTING –

KING.

WHAT ABOUT THE MARSHMALLOWS?

QUEEN.

WHO WANTS MARSHMALLOWS?

KING.

I DO.

QUEEN.

WHY?

KING.

FOR TOASTING!

STEWARD. *(Handing another list to the* **QUEEN.***)*

NOW IF IT PLEASE
YOUR MAJESTIES,
I HAVE A LIST OF WINE –
THE BEST OF ALL
THE VINTAGES
FROM EVERY NATION'S VINE.

KING. *(Querulously.)*

    I WANT THE WINE OF MY COUNTRY!

QUEEN.

    HUSH! HUSH! HUSH!

STEWARD.

    SHERRY AND PORT AND MUSCATEL,
    KIMMEL AND EAU DE VIE,
    DRY CHAMPAGNE AND SWEET MOSELLE,
    BURGUNDY AND CHABLIS,
    AQUAVIT AND LIEBFRAUMILCH,
    HOCK AND CHOCOLATE MALTED-MILCH,
    BRANDY, DRAMBUIE AND VODKA,
    WHITE AND CRYSTAL CLEAR!

KING. *(Rising with great determination.)*

    I WANT THE WINE OF MY COUNTRY!
    I WANT THE WINE OF MY COUNTRY!

> *(He throws out his arms expansively and the robe drops to the floor, revealing his belly bursting between the non-meeting trousers.)*

    I WANT THE WINE OF MY COUNTRY,
    THE WINE OF MY COUNTRY IS BEER!

> *(A button pops off his trousers and they fall to the floor.)*

QUEEN. Obviously!

[MUSIC NO. 07A "YOUR MAJESTIES (DANCE)"]

> *(The **CHEF** and **STEWARD** are joined by other **CHEFS**, **STEWARDS**, and **ASSISTANTS** until the stage is lined with men in white coats and tall white hats presenting in a dance every foodstuff known to man for the **KING** and **QUEEN**'s inspection. Other preparations for the ball – decorations, clothing, garlands, etc. – are also brought on by other members of the palace staff for royal approval. The dance builds to a rousing ending.)*

(After the applause, the **QUEEN** *ushers the line of staff members off the stage and gives the* **KING** *a final nod of her head as if to say, "So there." He remains seated, resigned to the inevitability of paying for and attending a ball he is not looking forward to.)*

PRINCE. *(Entering and crossing to the* **KING**.*)* Hello, Father.

KING. *(Turning around, as if having been awakened from a nap.)* Oh...uh...hello, my boy. Thought you were going for a ride.

PRINCE. I am, sir. The groom is bringing my horse around at three o'clock.

KING. Christopher, how are you feeling?

PRINCE. Fine, Father.

KING. *(Making it a leading question.)* You're not unhappy or anything – are you?

PRINCE. Why no, Father.

KING. *(Immediately comforted.)* That's what I thought.

(He beams.)

Ah! That's fine!

PRINCE. It seems to me, sir, that *you* look a little tired.

KING. *(Grouchily.)* I am tired, when I think of that darn ball.

(The **QUEEN** *enters, unseen by the* **MEN**. *She starts to cross to them, but stops when she hears the words about the ball. She steps back out of their sight lines, ready to get an earful.)*

You know, that ball you're giving – with my money.

PRINCE. Oh that. Well, to tell you the truth, sir, it isn't a night *I'm* looking forward to, dancing with all those... candidates.

KING. Candidates?

PRINCE. Every simpering girl in the Kingdom, each one determined to show that she would be the perfect princess for me.

KING. Yes, I know how you feel. More fun to chase one girl than to be stampeded by a whole herd of them!

PRINCE. One thing is sure: whoever I marry, it won't be anyone I meet at the ball!

KING. Know how you feel, my boy. I'd feel the same...only... there's one thing we mustn't forget. Your mother's got her heart set on giving this affair.

PRINCE. Yes, I know.

> *(The* **QUEEN** *starts as if about to go in and confront them.)*

KING. Uh... Christopher...

> *(The* **QUEEN** *stops and continues to listen.)*

If you talk to your mother about this, don't let her know how you feel. Tell her that you...that you love the idea of the ball. Know what I mean?
(Confidentially, man to man.) Make her feel good about it. Now I'll tell you...

> *(The* **QUEEN***, smiling, enters the room. The* **KING** *coughs to signal the* **PRINCE***.)*

Oh, hello, my dear. We... Christopher and I...were just...just...

PRINCE. I was just saying, Mother, how much I'm looking forward to the ball. It sounds wonderful.

QUEEN. *(Smiling.)* Does it?

PRINCE. Yes. I was wondering if I could help you at all... I mean in any of the preparations.

QUEEN. *(Pretending to be taken in by these fumbling men.)* Well, yes, dear. Maybe you can.

> *(There is a very awkward silence as she looks from one to the other, and neither knows what more to say about it, or how to carry the lie on any further.)*

PRINCE. *(Looking out the window.)* And I...I see they're bringing my horse around from the stables now.

*(He turns back and, on his way out of the
room, stops to kiss his MOTHER. Then, he waves
airily to his FATHER and exits. The QUEEN,
not offended by their deceit but touched by it,
blows her nose to hold back the tears in her
eyes.)*

KING. Have you got the sniffles? Getting a cold?

(The QUEEN shakes her head.)

Better take something for it.

(The QUEEN nods.)

Don't want to have a red nose at the ball.

(He chuckles at his own feeble joke.)

QUEEN. *(Getting the tears out of her voice.)* I'll be over it by
then.

(She gives her nose a good blow now.)

KING. Maisie...

QUEEN. What?

KING. That boy isn't unhappy.

QUEEN. How do you know?

KING. I asked him. He says he's feeling fine.

QUEEN. Did he?

(Smiling.)

You know something?

KING. What?

QUEEN. I love you.

*(She leans over the back of the KING's chair,
puts her arms around him, and kisses him
on the side of his head.)*

KING. *(With great dignity.)* Naturally you do. I'm the king.

QUEEN. Nothing to do with it.

[MUSIC NO. 08 "BOYS AND GIRLS LIKE YOU AND ME"]

QUEEN.

BOYS AND GIRLS LIKE YOU AND ME
WALK BENEATH THE SKIES.
THEY LOVE JUST AS WE LOVE,
WITH THE SAME DREAM IN THEIR EYES.
SONGS AND KINGS
AND MANY THINGS
HAVE THEIR DAY AND ARE GONE,
BUT BOYS AND GIRLS LIKE YOU AND ME,
WE GO ON AND ON.

KING.

THEY WALK ON EV'RY VILLAGE STREET,
THEY WALK IN LANES WHERE BRANCHES MEET,
AND STARS SEND DOWN THEIR BLESSINGS FROM THE
BLUE.

QUEEN.

THEY GO THROUGH STORMS OF DOUBT AND FEAR,
AND SO THEY GO FROM YEAR TO YEAR,
BELIEVING IN EACH OTHER AS WE DO,

KING & QUEEN.

BRAVELY MARCHING FORWARD, TWO BY TWO.

BOYS AND GIRLS
LIKE YOU AND ME

QUEEN.

WALK BENEATH THE SKIES.

KING.

THEY LOVE JUST AS WE LOVE,

QUEEN.

WITH THE SAME DREAM IN THEIR EYES.

KING & QUEEN.

SONGS AND KINGS
AND MANY THINGS
HAVE THEIR DAY AND ARE GONE,

BUT BOYS AND GIRLS LIKE YOU AND ME,
WE GO ON AND ON.

(They stroll off, arm in arm.)

(Blackout.)

(As the scene changes back to Cinderella's house, the **HERALD** *appears downstage and reads from a scroll.)*

[MUSIC NO. 09 "CHANGE OF SCENE"]

HERALD.

Hear ye, hear ye, hear ye all! A royal proclamation! A holiday is hereby proclaimed! Let every bank be closed!

(An unseen **CROWD** *cheers.)*

Let every shop be closed!

(Cheers.)

Let every school be closed!

(Shrill cheers from **CHILDREN**.*)*

Today is the day of the ball!

(Cheers.)

Scene Four

(Lights up on Cinderella's house. The **STEPMOTHER**, **JOY**, *and* **PORTIA** *are in the final stages of dressing for the ball. The following sequence again finds* **CINDERELLA** *meeting every demand with blinding speed and uncanny efficiency. This time she actually anticipates each new request and reaches for the article an instant before it is asked for.)*

STEPMOTHER. Cinderella! My gloves!

JOY. Cinderella, more curls!

PORTIA. Cinderella, more ribbons!

STEPMOTHER. Cinderella's no help at all...a very disorganized girl.

PORTIA. *(Pointing at* **CINDERELLA**, *she talks to the* **STEPMOTHER**.) Ma, no brains. When you haven't got it, you haven't got it. Cinderella hasn't got it!

JOY. Cinderella, my fan!

STEPMOTHER. Cinderella, my lorgnette!

JOY. Cinderella, my reticule!

PORTIA. Cinderella, my handkerchief!

CINDERELLA. *(Picking up three bouquets.)* The carriage is here! Oh, you all look so beautiful!

JOY. Yes, don't we?

STEPMOTHER. Cinderella, the flowers!

(She hands each a nosegay as she passes.)

Come along, girls.

(They exit.)

CINDERELLA. *(Calling after them, happily.)* Have a good time!

(Still smiling, she crosses to the fireplace.)

[MUSIC NO. 10 "IN MY OWN LITTLE CORNER (REPRISE) INTO FOL-DE-ROL"]

IN MY OWN LITTLE CORNER,
IN MY OWN LITTLE CHAIR,
I CAN BE WHATEVER I WANT TO BE.
ON THE WING OF MY FANCY
I CAN FLY ANYWHERE
AND THE WORLD WILL OPEN ITS ARMS TO ME.
I AM IN THE ROYAL PALACE, OF ALL PLACES!
I AM CHATTING WITH THE PRINCE AND KING AND
    QUEEN,
AND THE COLOR ON MY TWO STEPSISTERS' FACES
IS A QUEER SORT OF SOUR-APPLE GREEN!
I AM COY AND FLIRTATIOUS WHEN ALONE WITH THE
    PRINCE –

> *(She laughs flirtatiously as she imagines a
> conversation with the prince.)*

Ha, ha, ha! Oh, la, Your Highness, you shouldn't say
such things!

> *(The* **GODMOTHER** *appears at the window,
> unnoticed by* **CINDERELLA**.*)*

I'M THE BELLE OF THE BALL
IN MY OWN LITTLE CORNER,
ALL ALONE
IN MY OWN
LITTLE CHAIR.

> *(The* **GODMOTHER** *has watched everything.
> She is a sensible type of woman, showing no
> sign of any magic qualities. They come later.)*

Oh, I wish... I wish....

GODMOTHER.

FOL-DE-ROL AND FIDDLEDY DEE,
FIDDLEDY FADDLEDY FODDLE,
ALL THE WISHES IN ALL THE WORLD
ARE POPPYCOCK AND TWADDLE!

> *(***CINDERELLA*** *looks up on hearing her*
> ***GODMOTHER****'s voice and rushes to the
> window.)*

CINDERELLA. Godmother! I'm so glad to see you!

GODMOTHER. I thought you might be lonely, and I knew what you'd be doing.

CINDERELLA. What?

GODMOTHER. *(Singing to the strain of "In My Own Little Corner.")*

I JUST KNEW I WOULD FIND YOU

IN THAT SAME LITTLE CHAIR

IN THE PALE PINK MIST OF A FOOLISH DREAM.

CINDERELLA. What's wrong with that?

GODMOTHER.

FOL-DE-ROL AND FIDDLEDY DEE,

FIDDLEDY FADDLEDY FOODLE,

ALL THE DREAMERS IN ALL THE WORLD

ARE DIZZY IN THE NOODLE.

CINDERELLA. What do you suppose *every* girl is doing tonight? I mean every girl who isn't at the ball? She's dreaming and wishing she were really there.

GODMOTHER. But why aren't *you* really there?

CINDERELLA. My stepmother...well, somebody had to mind the house.

GODMOTHER. Do you know what I would do if I were you? I'd leave them. I'd just up and get out of the house. They make you work harder than a servant. If you want to be a servant, you can go to some other place and be paid.

CINDERELLA. You mean leave my stepmother? I don't think if Father were alive he would like that. Do you think so?

(Pause.)

GODMOTHER. Aren't you going to ask me in?

CINDERELLA. Oh, forgive me, Godmother...of course! Come round to the door.

(She crosses to the doorway. As her back is turned, there is a flash of light, and the

GODMOTHER *is standing calmly by the fireplace.)*

GODMOTHER. Don't bother.

*(***CINDERELLA*** *turns quickly, amazement on her face.)*

CINDERELLA. How did you get in?

GODMOTHER. *(Shrugs.)* The window.

CINDERELLA. *(Quite bewildered.)* The window.

GODMOTHER. The window. Aren't you going to offer me some tea?

(The fire suddenly lights by itself behind the **GODMOTHER,** *unseen by* **CINDERELLA.***)*

CINDERELLA. Oh, I'm terribly sorry... I'll just light the fire...

(She turns to the fireplace and sees the fire going.)

But it was out!

(She reaches out to touch the tea kettle but pulls her hand away quickly. Unseen by her, the **GODMOTHER** *motions to an empty vase on the kitchen table, and flowers appear in it.)*

And the kettle's hot! It's most curious...

(She turns and notices the flowers.)

Flowers! But I'm sure... *You* brought them, didn't you?

(She is very pleased to have solved at least this mystery.)

GODMOTHER. I thought they'd brighten the room. Your water's boiling.

CINDERELLA. *(Turning to fix the tea.)* Please sit down. I'll have this in a minute.

GODMOTHER. Thank you.

(She motions to a chair, and it moves across the floor until it is neatly under her and she sits.)

CINDERELLA. *(Bringing the tea, she sits next to the* **GODMOTHER**.*)* You know, I'm so awfully glad you happened to come by tonight. I *was* getting very lonely.

GODMOTHER. *(Wisely.)* I thought you might be.

CINDERELLA. *(Pouring tea.)* Godmother, do dreams never, *never* come true?

GODMOTHER. Oh, I wouldn't say never – just seldom.

CINDERELLA. That's not very often, is it?

GODMOTHER. Not very often is precisely what "seldom" is. You're a nice godchild, but you ask very foolish questions.

CINDERELLA. I wish you believed in wonderful things. I wish you believed that once in a while something marvelous and magical could happen.

GODMOTHER. *(Measuring her words.)* Well, I don't say that I *don't* believe that once in a while something marvelous and magical can't happen.

> *(She has picked up a small broom that had been propped up against the wall by the table.)*

CINDERELLA. For instance, do you believe in guardian angels?

GODMOTHER. *(Contemplating the broom.)* Well I-I, I can't say I *don't* believe in them.

> *(At this point, the end of the broom gleams like a shining star for a few seconds and then goes out. The* **GODMOTHER** *puts her hand on* **CINDERELLA**'*s head.)*

Only thing is, it's dangerous to believe too much in good fairies and guardian angels.

CINDERELLA. Why?

GODMOTHER. Oh, you get to lean on them too much. You get in the habit of sitting back and expecting them to do all the work for you. You've got to help yourself, you know.

CINDERELLA. I know. I think about it a lot, but then I don't know what to do. And so I always wind up just wishing and dreaming. I don't suppose *that* does any good at all.

GODMOTHER. Well, I don't say that it doesn't do any good at all. As a matter of fact, everything has to start with a wish. *Nothing* happens without wishing.

CINDERELLA. Do you know what I was wishing tonight? Just before you came?

GODMOTHER. *(Grimly.)* I'm almost afraid to hear.

CINDERELLA. *(Crossing to window.)* Do you see that pumpkin out in the yard?

GODMOTHER. I nearly stumbled over it in the dark.

CINDERELLA. The moon is shining on it now. Well, I was wishing that that pumpkin would turn into a great big royal golden carriage that would take me to the ball tonight.

GODMOTHER. What were you going to do for horses?

CINDERELLA. White mice. Four white mice would turn into horses! Beautiful white prancing steeds.

GODMOTHER. Were you going to drive them yourself?

CINDERELLA. Oh, no. There'd be a coachman and a footman and two flunkies on the back seat.

GODMOTHER. Where were *they* coming from?

CINDERELLA. They could be the four baby rats I saw down in the cellar yesterday.

(She looks up at her **GODMOTHER**.*)*

Oh, I know what you're going to say. Fol-de-rol and fiddledy dee.

GODMOTHER. Yes. Fol-de-rol and fiddledy dee!

CINDERELLA. It's impossible, I suppose.

GODMOTHER. Impossible.

CINDERELLA. Just the same, it was what I was wishing and I am still wishing it.

GODMOTHER. Nonsense.

CINDERELLA. I'm wishing it very hard.

GODMOTHER. You are?

CINDERELLA. Yes, I am.

(The end of the broom begins to shine again.)

[MUSIC NO. 11 "IMPOSSIBLE"]

CINDERELLA. If only I could have some magical help. If only I had a guardian angel or if my godmother were a Fairy Godmother.

GODMOTHER. Ha, ha! Good joke! Ho, ho! Very funny!

CINDERELLA. *(Very resolutely.)* I am wishing – in the name of every young girl who ever wanted to go to a dance and was told she couldn't – I am wishing that I may go to that dance tonight! I wish that, by some kind of magic or abracadabra or fol-de-rol and fiddledy dee, that all the kind hearts in the world will put their heads together...

GODMOTHER. All the kind hearts put their *heads* together?

CINDERELLA. You know what I mean...that all the kind hearts and good souls will wish with me and that you, Godmother, will help me with every ounce of strength and cleverness you possess!

GODMOTHER. *(Weakening, her voice softening.)* Cinderella...

CINDERELLA. *(Opening her eyes.)* Yes, Godmother?

(The **GODMOTHER,** *on the brink of giving in, becomes sensible again.)*

GODMOTHER. It's impossible!

CINDERELLA. *(Temporarily discouraged, her voice growing dull.)* Impossible. I suppose so.

GODMOTHER. *(As if making her last stand, she now sings.)*
IMPOSSIBLE
FOR A PLAIN YELLOW PUMPKIN TO BECOME A GOLDEN
    CARRIAGE!
IMPOSSIBLE
FOR A PLAIN COUNTRY BUMPKIN AND A PRINCE TO JOIN
    IN MARRIAGE,

AND FOUR WHITE MICE WILL NEVER BE FOUR WHITE
    HORSES –
SUCH FOL-DE-ROL AND FIDDLEDY DEE OF COURSE IS
    IMPOSSIBLE!
BUT THE WORLD IS FULL OF ZANIES AND FOOLS
WHO DON'T BELIEVE IN SENSIBLE RULES
AND WON'T BELIEVE WHAT SENSIBLE PEOPLE SAY,
AND BECAUSE THESE DAFT AND DEWY-EYED DOPES
KEEP BUILDING UP IMPOSSIBLE HOPES
IMPOSSIBLE THINGS ARE HAPPENING EVERY DAY!
IMPOSSIBLE!

CINDERELLA.

IMPOSSIBLE?

GODMOTHER.

IMPOSSIBLE!

CINDERELLA. *(Gloomily.)*

IMPOSSIBLE?

GODMOTHER.

IMPOSSIBLE!

CINDERELLA.

IMPOSSIBLE!

GODMOTHER & CINDERELLA.

IMPOSSIBLE!

    (Dialogue over music.)

CINDERELLA. "Impossible things are happening every day."
...Is that true, Godmother?

GODMOTHER. *(Grudgingly.)* Well, yes, I suppose so...in a
way.

CINDERELLA. Then I continue to build up my impossible
hope for tonight and I officially wish...

GODMOTHER. Officially wish?

CINDERELLA. I officially wish, and wish and wish all those
things I said about the pumpkin and the mice and the
rats.

GODMOTHER. Impossible!

CINDERELLA. *(Closing her eyes determinedly.)* Just the same, I'm wishing it!

GODMOTHER. *(Singing, but without her former conviction.)*
IMPOSSIBLE
FOR A PLAIN YELLOW PUMPKIN TO BECOME A GOLDEN
    CARRIAGE.
IMPOSSIBLE
FOR A PLAIN COUNTRY BUMPKIN AND A PRINCE TO JOIN
    IN MARRIAGE,
AND FOUR WHITE MICE WILL NEVER BE FOUR WHITE
    HORSES –

CINDERELLA. *(Shouting.)* They will!

GODMOTHER.
SUCH FOL-DE-ROL AND FIDDLEDY DEE OF COURSE IS
IMPOSSIBLE!

CINDERELLA. *(Singing earnestly, as if trying to sing her wish true.)*
BUT THE WORLD IS FULL OF ZANIES AND FOOLS
WHO DON'T BELIEVE IN SENSIBLE RULES
AND WON'T BELIEVE WHAT SENSIBLE PEOPLE SAY,

> *(The* **GODMOTHER,** *overwhelmed, joins her and sings with equal enthusiasm.)*

GODMOTHER & CINDERELLA.
AND BECAUSE THESE DAFT AND DEWY-EYED DOPES
KEEP BUILDING UP IMPOSSIBLE HOPES
IMPOSSIBLE THINGS ARE HAPPENING EVERY DAY.

[MUSIC NO. 12 "THE TRANSFORMATION"]

> *(The* **GODMOTHER** *waves her "broom wand," and the transformation begins. At designated moments in the music the house disappears,* **MICE** *dance on and become* **HORSES,** *the pumpkin turns into a magnificent golden carriage, and the* **FOOTMAN** *and* **COACHMAN** *appear with a gorgeous, full-length cape which they drape around* **CINDERELLA.** *[Optional: The carriage crossover can be done in silhouette.] They also place a tiara*

in her hair and ball slippers on her feet.
CINDERELLA's *eyes are closed, and she is*
unaware of what's happening.)

GODMOTHER. Cinderella... Look!

(She turns **CINDERELLA** *around.)*

CINDERELLA. G-g-g-Godmother! It's the coach and horses I wished for! And even the coachman and the footman!

(She turns to the **GODMOTHER.**)

But how?

(The **GODMOTHER** *smiles.)*

You?

GODMOTHER. *(Shrugging her shoulders.)* Fol-de-rol and fiddledy dee; it's magic.

CINDERELLA. *(Realizing that she has had the cape on.)* But... I don't understand...

GODMOTHER. ...And you don't have to. Come on! If you don't hurry, the ball will be over before you get there.

*(***CINDERELLA** *starts to the carriage, then runs to the* **GODMOTHER** *and hugs her.)*

CINDERELLA. Oh, Godmother, thank you! Thank you, it's wonderful!

(She walks slowly to the carriage, examining it in wonder, and sings to the **GODMOTHER.**)

[MUSIC NO. 13 "IT'S POSSIBLE (FINALE ACT I)"]

IT'S POSSIBLE
FOR A PLAIN YELLOW PUMPKIN TO BECOME A GOLDEN CARRIAGE.
IT'S POSSIBLE
FOR A PLAIN COUNTRY BUMPKIN AND A PRINCE TO JOIN IN MARRIAGE.

GODMOTHER.
AND FOUR WHITE MICE ARE EASILY TURNED TO HORSES!

CINDERELLA.

SUCH FOL-DE-ROL AND FIDDLEDY DEE OF COURSE IS
QUITE POSSIBLE!

(They start to get into the coach.)

GODMOTHER & CINDERELLA.

IT'S POSSIBLE!

CINDERELLA.

FOR THE WORLD IS FULL OF ZANIES AND FOOLS

GODMOTHER.

WHO DON'T BELIEVE IN SENSIBLE RULES

CINDERELLA.

AND WON'T BELIEVE WHAT SENSIBLE PEOPLE SAY.

GODMOTHER & CINDERELLA. *(Triumphantly.)*

AND BECAUSE THESE DAFT AND DEWY-EYED DOPES
KEEP BUILDING UP IMPOSSIBLE HOPES,
IMPOSSIBLE THINGS ARE HAPPENING EVERY DAY!

CINDERELLA.

IT'S POSSIBLE!

GODMOTHER.

IT'S POSSIBLE!

CINDERELLA.

IT'S POSSIBLE!

GODMOTHER.

IT'S POSSIBLE!

CINDERELLA.

IT'S POSSIBLE!

GODMOTHER.

IT'S POSSIBLE!

GODMOTHER & CINDERELLA.

IT'S POS-SI-BLE!

*(**CINDERELLA** and the **GODMOTHER** are now
seated in the carriage, and it carries them off
to the ball as the curtain falls.)*

ACT II

[MUSIC NO. 14 ENTR'ACTE"]

Scene One

[MUSIC NO. 15 "CURTAIN MUSIC ACT II"]

(Outside the palace. A clock in a tower in the distance clearly shows the time: 11:30. The **GODMOTHER** *enters with* **CINDERELLA.** *A* **FOOTMAN** *follows closely behind. The ball is in progress behind a scrim.)*

GODMOTHER. Now, you must go in and do exactly as I told you.

CINDERELLA. Aren't you coming with me?

GODMOTHER. Heavens, no. I've been to so many of these things *I* couldn't stand another. Furthermore, all I can do is give you your wish. How it turns out from here is up to you.

(Music fades out.)

CINDERELLA. But I'm afraid to go in there all by myself.

GODMOTHER. You needn't be except for one thing: Do not stay beyond twelve o'clock. See that you are in the coach and off for home before the clock strikes twelve.

CINDERELLA. Why is it so important that I leave before twelve?

GODMOTHER. You just obey and don't ask any questions.

CINDERELLA. But, Godmother...

(The **GODMOTHER** *disappears in a puff of smoke.)*

CINDERELLA. Where are you? Where did she go?

> *(The* **FOOTMAN** *just shrugs his shoulders.)*

She just...vanished out of sight! Did you ever see anything like that before?

FOOTMAN. Many times.

CINDERELLA. It's the first time *I've* seen it happen.

FOOTMAN. You'll see worse than that happen if you're not out of here before midnight.

CINDERELLA. *(Collects herself with a deep breath.)* I'm ready.

> *(They exit. The scrim raises and the scene changes to the ball in progress, but no one seems very excited with the proceedings, least of all the* **PRINCE.** *He is bored and obviously not interested in any of the* **LADIES** *being paraded by him.)*

[MUSIC NO. 16 "GAVOTTE"]

Scene Two

> *(Everyone dances to a stately and staid gavotte. Among the couples who dance by are* **JOY** *with a stout partner and* **PORTIA** *with a very short one whom she holds helpless in her embrace. The* **STEPMOTHER** *is dancing with a* **CLUMSY MAN.***)*

CLUMSY MAN. It's a long time since we danced together, Beulah!

STEPMOTHER. Not long enough.

> *(They dance away, she trying to escape both his company and his feet. The* **QUEEN** *leads in the* **KING.***)*

QUEEN. *(Beaming.)* Exhilarating, isn't it?

> *(The* **KING** *is unconvinced but gamely musters a smile.)*

Anyway, we are doing it for our son.

KING. I'm afraid he's having a worse time than I am. Look at him.

> *(They cross to their thrones on the side of the room, and the* **PRINCE** *dances center with a* **YOUNG GIRL** *who seems not to please him at all. A* **FOOTMAN** *comes toward him with another* **GIRL** *on his arm.)*

FOOTMAN. *(Presenting the* **GIRL.***)* Your Highness.

> *(The* **PRINCE** *bows to his partner, takes her, and dances off. As the* **FOOTMAN** *turns to go, we see the* **STEPMOTHER** *slipping money into his hand.)*

KING. *(Stage whisper.)* How long do you think we have to stay?

QUEEN. Until the very end.

(The **KING** *winces. The* **STEPMOTHER** *slips a bribe to one of the* **FOOTMEN,** *who takes* **JOY** *to the* **PRINCE.** **PORTIA,** *who hasn't seen this maneuver, crosses to the* **STEPMOTHER.***)*

PORTIA. I've lost track of the Prince. Where is he?

STEPMOTHER. He's dancing with Joy.

PORTIA. *(Brightly.)* He is?

*(***STEPMOTHER** *points,* **PORTIA**'*s face changes.)*

Oh, *that* Joy. I want a chance at him.

STEPMOTHER. You shall have it.

(She crooks her finger at another **FOOTMAN,** *who approaches, and she takes money for him out of her purse, speaking to* **PORTIA** *at the same time.)*

Remember what I told you. Beauty is not enough. You must show him you have brains, like your namesake, Portia, in *The Merchant of Venice.*

(The **PRINCE** *has danced into the scene with* **JOY.** *Two more joyless people would be hard to imagine.* **PORTIA** *dashes from her* **STEPMOTHER** *to the* **PRINCE**'*s side. She tries to bombard him with her conversation, while* **JOY** *keeps trying to block her view.)*

PORTIA. *(To the* **PRINCE.***)* Do you know what I want to be? A lawyer!

(The **PRINCE** *nods politely, taking this information in his stride.)*

Someday I'll stand up in the courtroom...

[MUSIC NO. 17 "CINDERELLA'S ENTRANCE"]

*(***CINDERELLA** *appears at the top of the steps. She is now dressed in a stunning, shimmering ballgown, absolutely beautiful from head to toe. The* **PRINCE** *turns his head and sees her.)*

(Continues talking, although the **PRINCE** *is obviously distracted.)* ...And I'll say to some old judge or something about how like the quality of mercy is not strained, know what I mean? I'll say it splashes down like the dew from...heaven?

> *(During* **PORTIA***'s speech, groups of* **GUESTS** *stop dancing as they notice* **CINDERELLA** *at the top of the stairs.* **PORTIA***, of course, is the last to notice, but finally she too falls silent. Everyone stands like a statue, holding their breath as* **CINDERELLA** *descends the stairs, and the* **PRINCE***, like a man in a trance, moves to meet her at the bottom. There, he bows and she curtsies. He offers his arm, she takes it, and the dance continues, this time with a bit more spirit. After a moment, the silence of the* **GUESTS** *is shattered, and suddenly everyone in the room is buzzing with excitement and curiosity, everyone asking, "Who is she?")*

KING. Now the party is beginning to look better!

QUEEN. I wonder who she is.

> *(The* **GUESTS** *continue asking each other, "Who is she?" but no one seems to know.)*

All of a sudden he is a different boy! His face has lighted up. He is dancing with a new spring in his step.

KING. Watching him dance with that lovely creature – you know, it takes me back.

QUEEN. To where?

KING. To the first time I danced with you, my darling.

QUEEN. I wonder who she is.

STEPMOTHER. *(From other side of stage.)* I wonder who she is.

PORTIA. Who is she?

JOY. I never saw the girl before.

STEPMOTHER. Well, whoever she is, it's clear to me he likes *her* the best.

PORTIA. Funny. She doesn't look very intellectual.

> (**JOY** *gives her sister the kind of look this*
> *remark deserves. The dance goes on. As it*
> *does, the* **PRINCE** *leads* **CINDERELLA** *out into*
> *the garden. The scrim descends. The clock in*
> *the tower now shows it to be 11:40.)*

Scene Three

PRINCE. I have never met you before, have I?

CINDERELLA. No... I don't get out much.

PRINCE. I don't even know your name.

> (**CINDERELLA** *just smiles.*)

Mine is Christopher.

CINDERELLA. Yes. I know – Christopher Rupert Windemere Vladimir Karl...

PRINCE. I don't use all those names. I would like you to call me just Christopher.

CINDERELLA. *(Overwhelmed.)* You would?

> *(The* **PRINCE** *nods. Then, after a pause, he speaks again.)*

[MUSIC NO. 18 "TEN MINUTES AGO"]

PRINCE. Have you a strange feeling that something has just happened to you and you don't know what it is?

CINDERELLA. Yes, that is exactly the way I feel.

PRINCE. And you have no idea what it may be?

> (**CINDERELLA** *opens her mouth to answer honestly and eagerly, but thinks better of it.)*

CINDERELLA. ...No, I have no idea.

> *(Shyly.)* I wonder how we can find out...what...it is.

PRINCE. Let us think back over our history together.

CINDERELLA. It isn't very long, is it?

> *(The* **PRINCE** *smiles and shakes his head, and then he starts to sing.)*

PRINCE.

TEN MINUTES AGO I SAW YOU.
I LOOKED UP WHEN YOU CAME THROUGH THE DOOR.
MY HEAD STARTED REELING,
YOU GAVE ME THE FEELING
THE ROOM HAD NO CEILING OR FLOOR.
TEN MINUTES AGO I MET YOU,

AND WE MURMURED OUR HOW-DO-YOU-DOS.
I WANTED TO RING OUT
THE BELLS AND FLING OUT
MY ARMS AND TO SING OUT THE NEWS:
I HAVE FOUND HER!
SHE'S AN ANGEL,
WITH THE DUST OF THE STARS IN HER EYES!
WE ARE DANCING,
WE ARE FLYING
AND SHE'S TAKING ME BACK TO THE SKIES.
IN THE ARMS OF MY LOVE I'M FLYING
OVER MOUNTAIN AND MEADOW AND GLEN,
AND I LIKE IT SO WELL
THAT FOR ALL I CAN TELL
I MAY NEVER COME DOWN AGAIN!
I MAY NEVER COME DOWN TO EARTH AGAIN!

I have told you how I felt. You haven't described your feelings.

CINDERELLA. Well, they're very much the same as yours.
TEN MINUTES AGO I MET YOU,
AND WE MURMURED OUR HOW-DO-YOU-DOS.
I WANTED TO RING OUT
THE BELLS AND FLING OUT
MY ARMS AND TO SING OUT THE NEWS:
I HAVE FOUND HIM! I HAVE FOUND HIM –

> (*The* **PRINCE** *now takes her in his arms, and they dance for several measures of the refrain.*)

IN THE ARMS OF MY LOVE I'M FLYING
OVER MOUNTAIN AND MEADOW AND GLEN,
AND I LIKE IT SO WELL
THAT FOR ALL I CAN TELL
I MAY NEVER COME DOWN AGAIN!

CINDERELLA & PRINCE.
I MAY NEVER COME DOWN TO EARTH AGAIN!

PRINCE. May I show you around the Royal Gardens?

CINDERELLA. I would like that very much.

(The **PRINCE** *offers* **CINDERELLA** *his arm. She accepts, and they exit. As they go off right, the two* **STEPSISTERS** *enter left in great indignation. They haven't been eavesdropping long, but just the picture of* **CINDERELLA** *and the* **PRINCE** *walking off arm-in-arm is enough to set them off.)*

[MUSIC NO. 19 "STEPSISTERS' LAMENT"]

JOY.

WHY WOULD A FELLOW WANT A GIRL LIKE HER,
A FRAIL AND FLUFFY BEAUTY?
WHY CAN'T A FELLOW EVER ONCE PREFER
A SOLID GIRL LIKE ME?

PORTIA.

SHE'S A FROTHY LITTLE BUBBLE
WITH A FLIMSY KIND OF CHARM,
AND WITH VERY LITTLE TROUBLE
I COULD BREAK HER LITTLE ARM!

JOY.

OH, OH, WHY WOULD A FELLOW WANT A GIRL LIKE HER,
SO OBVIOUSLY UNUSUAL?
WHY CAN'T A FELLOW EVER ONCE PREFER
A USUAL GIRL LIKE ME?

PORTIA.

HER FACE IS EXQUISITE, I SUPPOSE
BUT NO MORE EXQUISITE THAN A ROSE IS.

JOY.

HER SKIN MAY BE DELICATE AND SOFT
BUT NOT ANY SOFTER THAN A DOE'S IS.

PORTIA.

HER NECK IS NO LONGER THAN A SWAN'S.

JOY.

SHE'S ONLY AS DAINTY AS A DAISY.

PORTIA.

SHE'S ONLY AS GRACEFUL AS A BIRD.

PORTIA & JOY.

SO WHY IS THE FELLOW GOING CRAZY?

OH, WHY WOULD A FELLOW WANT A GIRL LIKE HER,
A GIRL WHO'S MERELY LOVELY?
WHY CAN'T A FELLOW EVER ONCE PREFER
A GIRL WHO'S MERELY ME?
WHAT'S THE MATTER WITH THE MAN?
WHAT'S THE MATTER WITH THE MAN?
WHAT'S THE MATTER WITH THE MAN?

(They exit, one offstage right and the other offstage left. The scrim is now taken out and we are back at the ball.)

[MUSIC NO. 20 "WALTZ FOR A BALL (CINDERELLA WALTZ)"]

Scene Four

(The music begins, and we are swept back into the ballroom for the Grand Waltz. There is a decidely different air this time – everyone has been caught up into the romantic mood of the waltz. The stage is filled with swirls of people, color, and electricity. Things are looking up.)

(After the first section of music, the **COMPANY** *breaks into a reprise of "Ten Minutes Ago," which signals the sweeping entrance of* **CINDERELLA** *and the* **PRINCE**.*)*

COMPANY.
TEN MINUTES AGO I SAW YOU;
I LOOKED UP WHEN YOU CAME THROUGH THE DOOR.
MY HEAD STARTED REELING,
YOU GAVE ME THE FEELING
THE ROOM HAD NO CEILING OR FLOOR.
TEN MINUTES AGO I MET YOU,
AND WE MURMURED OUR HOW-DO-YOU-DOS.
I WANTED TO RING OUT
THE BELLS AND FLING OUT
MY ARMS AND TO SING OUT THE NEWS:
I HAVE FOUND HER!
SHE'S AN ANGEL,
WITH THE DUST OF THE STARS IN HER EYES!
WE ARE DANCING,
WE ARE FLYING
AND SHE'S TAKING ME BACK TO THE SKIES.
IN THE ARMS OF MY LOVE I'M FLYING
OVER MOUNTAIN AND MEADOW AND GLEN,
AND I LIKE IT SO WELL
THAT FOR ALL I CAN TELL
I MAY NEVER COME DOWN AGAIN!
I MAY NEVER COME DOWN TO EARTH AGAIN!

(Now **CINDERELLA** *and the* **PRINCE** *are the focus of the waltz, while* **GUESTS** *continue to dance and sing. The* **KING** *and* **QUEEN** *come down from their seats and cut in on the* **PRINCE** *and* **CINDERELLA,** *the* **KING** *dancing with* **CINDERELLA** *and the* **QUEEN** *with her son. All the while, the* **STEPMOTHER** *is trying to find a suitable partner for herself, and* **JOY** *and* **PORTIA** *end up dancing with each other. After several bars, the* **PRINCE** *hands the* **QUEEN** *back to the* **KING** *and takes* **CINDERELLA** *in his arms. They all waltz around the room, bringing the dance to a grand and glorious finish.)*

[MUSIC NO. 21 "WALTZ (UNDERSCORE)"]

PRINCE. The ballroom is too crowded.

CINDERELLA. It's nicer out here.

PRINCE. Yes, it is, with the moon beaming down on us.

(They are looking up at the moon, together. The time is 11:50. Suddenly, **CINDERELLA** *realizes she has to leave.)*

PRINCE. What is the matter?

CINDERELLA. I must go!

PRINCE. Why?

CINDERELLA. Because I...I promised my godmother.

PRINCE. Your godmother will forgive you if you're a little late.

CINDERELLA. Oh, no, she won't. You don't understand...I have a strange kind of godmother.

PRINCE. You're a strange kind of girl. You haven't yet told me your name.

(Pause.)

CINDERELLA. It's a silly name. You wouldn't like it.

PRINCE. Of course I would. Whatever you are called is the most beautiful name in the world.

(He takes her hand.)

Whatever your name is... I love you... I will always love you.

> *(**CINDERELLA** looks up at him, and the clock fades from her mind.)*

You don't say anything. I have just told you that I love you and you don't say anything.

CINDERELLA. I'm afraid to. I'm afraid I might wake up.

PRINCE. Are you sure you are asleep?

CINDERELLA. Oh, yes!

PRINCE. Are you dreaming that I am about to kiss you?

> *(This is going too fast for **CINDERELLA**. She can't think of an answer. The **PRINCE** takes her in his arms gently. It is a slow, shy, not very long, but very important kiss.)*

It is strange how things happen. A girl I never saw before comes down a flight of stairs and my whole life is changed. Suddenly I am in a different world. I am deeply in love, and yet I don't know *why* I am in love, do you?

CINDERELLA. Do I what?

PRINCE. Do you know why I am in love?

> *(**CINDERELLA** shakes her head and smiles.)*

What did you think I meant?

CINDERELLA. I thought you meant, do I know why *I* am in love.

PRINCE. Well, do you? I mean are you?

CINDERELLA. Oh, yes.

PRINCE. And do you know why?

CINDERELLA. No, but I don't care why.

PRINCE. I always want to know *why* I do anything, why I feel anything. And so I ask myself why you, a stranger, are suddenly the only kind of girl I could love, and you are the only one of your kind. Why? Why is the sound of your voice the sweetest sound in the world? Why is the color of your hair the only color a girl's hair should be? Why would I rather hold you in my arms than do anything else in the world? Why?

CINDERELLA. Because, Your Highnessss...

PRINCE. Christopher.

[MUSIC NO. 22 "DO I LOVE YOU BECAUSE YOU'RE BEAUTIFUL?"]

CINDERELLA. Christopher...because that's the way you feel.

PRINCE. But why do I feel that way? What makes you so miraculous?

CINDERELLA. *(Smiling.)* Your imagination.

PRINCE. Then what makes my imagination so miraculous?

> (**CINDERELLA** *laughs and shakes her head to indicate she doesn't know, but she seems to be loving every minute of the interview just the same. The* **PRINCE** *starts to sing.*)

DO I LOVE YOU
BECAUSE YOU'RE BEAUTIFUL?
OR ARE YOU BEAUTIFUL
BECAUSE I LOVE YOU?
AM I MAKING BELIEVE I SEE IN YOU
A GIRL TOO LOVELY TO
BE REALLY TRUE?
DO I WANT YOU
BECAUSE YOU'RE WONDERFUL?
OR ARE YOU WONDERFUL
BECAUSE I WANT YOU?
ARE YOU THE SWEET INVENTION OF A LOVER'S DREAM,
OR ARE YOU REALLY AS BEAUTIFUL AS YOU SEEM?

> (**CINDERELLA** *and the* **PRINCE** *gaze into each other's eyes.* **CINDERELLA** *speaks over the music of the second refrain as it starts.*)

CINDERELLA. Maybe you do just imagine me. Maybe I am imagining you...

AM I MAKING BELIEVE I SEE IN YOU
A MAN TOO PERFECT TO BE REALLY TRUE?

DO I WANT YOU BECAUSE YOU'RE WONDERFUL?
OR ARE YOU WONDERFUL BECAUSE I WANT YOU?

CINDERELLA & PRINCE.

ARE YOU THE SWEET INVENTION OF A LOVER'S DREAM,
OR ARE YOU REALLY
AS WONDERFUL AS YOU SEEM?

(When the song finishes, the **PRINCE** *starts to gather* **CINDERELLA** *in his arms again.)*

PRINCE. Now tell me your name.

*(***CINDERELLA** *is about to when...)*

[MUSIC NO. 23 "TWELVE O'CLOCK"]

CINDERELLA. *(Pulling away from him.)* The clock!

(The **PRINCE** *turns to look at the clock, which is striking twelve, and in that moment* **CINDERELLA** *pulls away from him and dashes off.)*

(The **PRINCE** *turns back to her, but she is gone! He catches a glimpse of her running through the crowd as the scene changes back to the ballroom. He dashes through the crowd after her, but is intercepted again and again by people trying to greet him or stop him. He brushes past them as quickly as he can, but they are too many for him.)*

*(***CINDERELLA** *arrives at the top of the stairs, stumbles for a moment, then regains her footing and dashes out. Finally, the* **PRINCE** *makes his way to the top of the stairs, but* **CINDERELLA** *is gone. He looks down and sees something on the ground in front of him. He bends down, and, on a chord from the orchestra, he picks the object up. It is the glass slipper.)*

(He stands alone, puzzled, dejected, and defeated as the curtain falls.)

(Curtain.)

ACT III

[MUSIC NO. 24 "PRELUDE TO ACT III (CINDERELLA MARCH – COMPLETE)"]

Scene One

[MUSIC NO. 25 "CURTAIN MUSIC ACT III"]

(Cinderella's house. It is the morning after the ball. The **STEPMOTHER**, **JOY**, *and* **PORTIA** *in their dressing gowns are having a late breakfast.* **CINDERELLA** *is of course cooking and serving them during the scene.)*

STEPMOTHER. What a night! What a magnificent affair.

CINDERELLA. *(Playing innocent.)* Were there many people there?

STEPMOTHER. Oh, I should say about five thousand.

(Turning to her daughters.)

What would you say, girls?

PORTIA. I would say about ten thousand.

JOY. Or twelve!

CINDERELLA. It must be a very large ballroom at the palace.

JOY. About a half a mile long.

STEPMOTHER. And what beautiful music for dancing!

CINDERELLA. Did you dance, too?

STEPMOTHER. I should say I did! I met an old beau of mine, and he practically monopolized me.

CINDERELLA. Was he a good dancer?

STEPMOTHER. Light as a feather.

(The **STEPMOTHER** *stops massaging her feet and inserts them in the bucket of hot water* **CINDERELLA** *has filled in front of her.)*

CINDERELLA. Did any of you get to dance with the prince?

JOY. Did any of us get to dance with the prince?

PORTIA. Did you hear what she said? Did we get to dance! I danced about an hour with him.

JOY. You danced about an hour with him?

PORTIA. Didn't *you*?

JOY. Well, of course I did, if *you* did.

CINDERELLA. Did you know everyone there?

STEPMOTHER. Nearly everyone. All except a princess who came in very late and left very early. I had no idea who she was.

CINDERELLA. *(Interested and stopping whatever she is doing at the moment.)* Did *she* dance with the prince?

PORTIA. Y-y-yes. I think I saw her dancing with him once.

JOY. That's right, just once.

CINDERELLA. Do you think he liked her?

JOY. *(Making a noise that means yes and no or so-so.)* N-n-yeh.

STEPMOTHER. She was only there for a few minutes.

JOY. Did you go to sleep right after we left?

CINDERELLA. No. I stayed up till...a little after midnight.

STEPMOTHER. What were you doing all that time?

CINDERELLA. Dreaming.

STEPMOTHER. Dreaming what?

CINDERELLA. Oh, what it must be like at the ball.

STEPMOTHER. You couldn't possibly dream what it was like unless you were there.

CINDERELLA. Well, I was trying to.

JOY. Well, you just couldn't.

CINDERELLA. Maybe I have more imagination than you think. I have been dreaming and trying to feel just the way you must feel – the way all girls must be feeling – looking forward to the ball all that time and finally *the* night arrives, and you put on the most beautiful dress you have ever worn in your life...and off you go! I think I can almost feel what it's like. I imagine... I imagine...

(In high excitement she starts to sing.)

[MUSIC NO. 26 "WHEN YOU'RE DRIVING THROUGH THE MOONLIGHT"]

WHEN YOU'RE DRIVING THROUGH THE MOONLIGHT ON THE HIGHWAY,
WHEN YOU'RE DRIVING THROUGH THE MOONLIGHT TO THE DANCE,
YOU ARE BREATHLESS WITH A WILD ANTICIPATION
OF ADVENTURE AND EXCITEMENT AND ROMANCE.
THEN AT LAST YOU SEE THE TOWERS OF THE PALACE
SILHOUETTED ON THE SKY ABOVE THE PARK,
AND BELOW THEM IS A ROW OF LIGHTED WINDOWS,
LIKE A LOVELY DIAMOND NECKLACE IN THE DARK!

PORTIA.

IT LOOKS THAT WAY –

JOY.

THE WAY YOU SAY.

STEPMOTHER. *(Puzzled and vaguely suspicious.)*

SHE TALKS AS IF SHE KNOWS.

CINDERELLA. *(Tactfully.)*

I DO NOT KNOW THESE THINGS ARE SO.
I ONLY JUST SUPPOSE...
I SUPPOSE THAT WHEN YOU COME INTO THE BALLROOM,
AND THE ROOM ITSELF IS FLOATING IN THE AIR,
IF YOU'RE SUDDENLY CONFRONTED BY HIS HIGHNESS
YOU ARE FROZEN LIKE A STATUE ON THE STAIR!
YOU'RE AFRAID HE'LL HEAR THE WAY YOUR HEART IS BEATING
AND YOU KNOW YOU MUSTN'T MAKE THE FIRST ADVANCE.
YOU ARE SERIOUSLY THINKING OF RETREATING –
THEN YOU SEEM TO HEAR HIM ASKING YOU TO DANCE!
YOU MAKE A BOW

A TIMID BOW
AND SHYLY ANSWER "YES" –

STEPMOTHER.
HOW WOULD YOU KNOW
THAT THIS IS SO?

CINDERELLA. *(Humbly.)*
I DO NO MORE THAN GUESS.

JOY & PORTIA. *(Singing loud, like two very devout choir singers.)*
YOU CAN GUESS TILL YOU'RE BLUE IN THE FACE
BUT YOU CAN'T EVEN PICTURE SUCH A MAN.

JOY.
HE IS *MORE* THAN A PRINCE –

PORTIA.
HE'S AN *ACE*!

CINDERELLA.
BUT SISTERS, I REALLY THINK I CAN –

STEPMOTHER. Can what?

CINDERELLA.
I THINK THAT I CAN PICTURE SUCH A MAN...

JOY & PORTIA. *(Reverently starting to sing a hymn to his charms.)*
HE IS TALL –

CINDERELLA.
AND STRAIGHT AS A LANCE!

JOY & PORTIA.
AND HIS HAIR –

CINDERELLA.
IS DARK AND WAVY.

JOY & PORTIA.
HIS EYES –

CINDERELLA.
CAN MELT YOU WITH A GLANCE!

JOY & PORTIA.
HE CAN TURN A GIRL TO GRAVY!

*(Underneath the following spoken dialogue,
the reprise melody of "Ten Minutes Ago.")*

CINDERELLA. When he waltzes he whirls you around so that
your feet never touch the floor.

PORTIA. That's right, they don't!

CINDERELLA. And he makes you feel that you weigh nothing
at all.

JOY. That's right, he does!

CINDERELLA. He leads you around the crowded ballroom,
then out onto the terrace...

PORTIA. That's right...

JOY. He does?

PORTIA. Didn't he lead *you* out onto the terrace?

JOY. I guess he did. I was so faint with joy I didn't know
what was happening to me.

PORTIA. Me, too.

CINDERELLA. Out on the terrace...

*(The **STEPMOTHER** and the two **SISTERS** are all
ears now, leaning forward, under the spell.)*

...you stop dancing.

JOY. Yes?

CINDERELLA. You walk.

PORTIA. Yes?

CINDERELLA. You stop walking.

JOY. Y-yes?

CINDERELLA. You talk...

*(By now the other three **WOMEN** are completely
under the same spell of romance as **CINDERELLA**,
and they listen with wide eyes and beautiful
faces.)*

Then...

PORTIA. You stop talking?

CINDERELLA. That's right.

JOY. Then...?

CINDERELLA. You start thinking!

JOY. *(As if this makes everything clear.)* Oh.

> *(She then realizes she still doesn't understand.)*

PORTIA. *(Who never made any pretense of understanding.)* Start thinking what?

CINDERELLA. Thinking...how wonderful it all is!

STEPMOTHER. How wonderful *what* all is?

CINDERELLA. Everything.

> *(She is as dreamy-eyed with memories as only someone it had actually happened to can be.)*

[MUSIC NO. 27 "A LOVELY NIGHT"]

A LOVELY NIGHT,
A LOVELY NIGHT,
A FINER NIGHT YOU KNOW YOU'LL NEVER SEE.
YOU MEET YOUR PRINCE,
A CHARMING PRINCE,
AS CHARMING AS A PRINCE WILL EVER BE!
THE STARS IN A HAZY HEAVEN
TREMBLE ABOVE YOU
WHILE HE IS WHISPERING,
"DARLING, I LOVE YOU!"
YOU SAY GOODBYE,
AWAY YOU FLY,
BUT ON YOUR LIPS YOU KEEP A KISS,
ALL YOUR LIFE YOU'LL DREAM OF THIS
LOVELY, LOVELY NIGHT.

> *(The **STEPMOTHER**, **JOY**, and **PORTIA** have momentarily forgotten their disdain for **CINDERELLA** and have gotten wrapped up in her description. **CINDERELLA** has her family audience in the palm of her hand.)*

> *(Then the **STEPMOTHER** and the two **SISTERS**, as they do with everything else, try to take over. They act out the fantasy the way it should happen – to them! **CINDERELLA** watches with*

a friendly smile, genuinely entertained.
Where her version was full of romance and
hope, the version we see now is filled with
laughs, accompanied by, among other things,
a ricky-tick piano.)

PORTIA.

A LOVELY NIGHT,

A LOVELY NIGHT,

JOY. *(Her deadpan sourness contrasting with* **PORTIA**'s
intolerable effervescence.)

A FINER NIGHT YOU KNOW YOU'LL NEVER SEE.

STEPMOTHER.

YOU MEET YOUR PRINCE,

A CHARMING PRINCE,

JOY.

AS CHARMING AS A PRINCE WILL EVER BE!

PORTIA.

THE STARS IN A HAZY HEAVEN

TREMBLE ABOVE YOU

JOY.

WHILE HE IS WHISPERING,

PORTIA.

"DARLING, I LOVE YOU!"

STEPMOTHER.

YOU SAY GOODBYE,

AWAY YOU FLY,

JOY.

BUT ON YOUR LIPS YOU KEEP A KISS

PORTIA.

ALL YOUR LIFE YOU'LL DREAM OF THIS

STEPMOTHER, PORTIA & JOY.

LOVELY, LOVELY NIGHT.

(The three are so pleased with their
presentation and themselves that they launch
into a kind of encore. They grow quite carried
away with it all and march about the room

in a broad and absurd parody of themselves.
Perhaps in their minds' eyes, they are even
more beautiful – but to ours, they are only
funnier. **CINDERELLA** *sits and watches with*
genuine delight, obviously happy that they
are having such a good time.)

PORTIA.

A LOVELY NIGHT

JOY. *(Trying to upstage her, as usual.)* "How lovely!"

PORTIA. *(Doing the same.)*

A LOVELY NIGHT

JOY. "How lovely!"

PORTIA.

A FINER NIGHT YOU KNOW YOU'LL NEVER SEE.

JOY. "How lovely!"

PORTIA.

SHUSH! YOU MEET...

JOY.

...YOUR PRINCE!

PORTIA.

A CHARM...

JOY.

...ING PRINCE!

STEPMOTHER.

AS CHARMING AS A PRINCE WILL EVER BE!
THE STARS IN A HAZY HEAVEN...

JOY.

...TREMBLE ABOVE YOU

STEPMOTHER.

WHILE HE IS WHISPERING...

PORTIA.

"DARLING, I LOVE YOU!"

STEPMOTHER.

YOU SAY GOODBYE,
AWAY YOU FLY,

JOY.

> BUT ON YOUR LIPS YOU KEEP A KISS...

PORTIA.

> ...ALL YOUR LIFE YOU'LL DREAM OF THIS

STEPMOTHER, PORTIA & JOY.

> LOVELY, LOVELY NIGHT.

> *(They all sigh deeply and hold the picture for a moment. When the applause is over, a decidedly more peaceful version of the song begins as an underscore to the following dialogue. The* **STEPMOTHER** *suddenly becomes conscious of what has been done to her and she becomes her old self.)*

[MUSIC NO. 28 "A LOVELY NIGHT (CODA)"]

STEPMOTHER. Worst nonsense I ever heard! Rubbish and drivel!

> *(Turning on her two* **DAUGHTERS***.)*

And you, listening to her...and even aping her very words!

JOY. But Mother...

STEPMOTHER. Enough! Go to your room!

PORTIA. *(As she and* **JOY** *exit.)* It's all Cinderella's fault.

JOY. Imagine her trying to imagine what it was like at the ball.

PORTIA. It wasn't anything like that.

JOY. Nothing like it at all.

PORTIA. You know what they always say –

JOY. An idle mind is the devil's workshop.

PORTIA. That's what they always say.

STEPMOTHER. *(Turning to* **CINDERELLA***.)* And you, clean this place up. It looks like a pig pen!

CINDERELLA. *(Meekly.)* Yes, ma'am.

> *(The* **STEPMOTHER** *exits.* **CINDERELLA** *goes straight over to her own little corner, sits in her own little chair, and muses.)*

(She picks up the broom and sings the following as if the broom were the prince.)

CINDERELLA.
THE STARS IN A HAZY HEAVEN
TREMBLING ABOVE ME,
DANCED WHEN HE PROMISED
ALWAYS TO LOVE ME.
THE DAY CAME THROUGH,
AWAY I FLEW,
BUT ON MY LIPS HE LEFT A KISS –
ALL MY LIFE I'LL DREAM OF THIS LOVELY, LOVELY NIGHT.

(Blackout.)

Scene Two

[MUSIC NO. 29 "DO I LOVE YOU (UNDERSCORE)"]

(The scene now changes to the royal dressing room. The KING *and* QUEEN *stand together, listening to the* PRINCE. *The* HERALD *stands slightly behind the* PRINCE, *holding in his hands a cushion upon which sits the glass slipper.)*

PRINCE. I know it belongs to her.

KING. What are you going to do?

(Pause.)

PRINCE. Sir, may I have your royal guards to send through the kingdom in search of her?

KING. Of course you may.

PRINCE. And your secret service, may I call them in to help me?

KING. Yes, of course. They never find out anything, but you can try.

PRINCE. I will try everything! I will search every inch of the kingdom for the owner of this slipper.

KING. *(Looking at the slipper.)* That's what *I* would do.

(He breaks out of his reverie to see the QUEEN *staring at him. He speaks to her.)*

Well, I would.

PRINCE. *(Speaking to the* HERALD.*)* See that the slipper is tried on every young girl in the kingdom, every last one no matter how unlikely she looks. You are to keep trying until you find the one that fits. Do you understand?

HERALD. Yes, sir!

PRINCE. Find that girl!

(The HERALD *bows and exits. The* QUEEN *signals to the* KING *that he should leave, too.)*

KING. I will...just...go speak with the chief of my secret service.

(*He exits.*)

QUEEN. Chris...

(*The* **PRINCE** *has been lost in thought, but now looks up.*)

Suppose you *don't* find her.

PRINCE. I *must* find her.

QUEEN. Before last night you knew nothing about her. You know nothing about her now except that she danced prettily and that she looked pretty.

PRINCE. I know that she's the loveliest thing on Earth, and I will never be happy without her.

QUEEN. Why do you think that?

PRINCE. I don't know *why*...and I don't expect you to understand, Mother.

QUEEN. But I do understand, Chris. I know it doesn't take long to...to feel the way you do about this girl.

(*The* **PRINCE** *gives her a quick look.*)

But there is one fact I want you to face. You may never see her again... I don't want you to waste your life on a dream. I want you to be in love with a real girl.

PRINCE. She is real.

QUEEN. She was real last night. If she doesn't come back, she will never be real again, will she?

(*The* **PRINCE** *turns away.*)

Chris...be honest with yourself. Does your future happiness really depend upon your finding her? Or are you telling yourself that? Don't be angry with me. Think over what I am saying. Ask yourself if this is not just an illusion, an infatuation with something that doesn't exist at all.

(*She looks deeply concerned, worried, and sympathetic, too. But she realizes that she can only do so much and that the* **PRINCE** *must decide his future for himself.)*

PRINCE. *(Walking away from his* **MOTHER** *to the window, addressing a Cinderella who is not there.)* You're somewhere out there. I don't know where. You said last night that you thought we were dreaming. Maybe you were right. Maybe my mother is right.

[MUSIC NO. 30 "DO I LOVE YOU BECAUSE YOU'RE BEAUTIFUL? (REPRISE)"]

How can I know? How can one ever know?

DO I LOVE YOU
BECAUSE YOU'RE BEAUTIFUL?

QUEEN. *(About ten feet away from him.)*

OR IS SHE BEAUTIFUL
BECAUSE YOU LOVE HER?

PRINCE.

AM I MAKING BELIEVE I SEE IN YOU
A GIRL TOO LOVELY TO
BE REALLY TRUE?
DO I WANT YOU
BECAUSE YOU'RE WONDERFUL?

QUEEN.

OR IS SHE WONDERFUL
BECAUSE YOU WANT HER?

PRINCE.

ARE YOU THE SWEET INVENTION OF A LOVER'S DREAM?
OR ARE YOU REALLY AS BEAUTIFUL AS YOU SEEM?

(The lights fade out on the scene.)

Scene Three

[MUSIC NO. 31 "THE SEARCH"]

(The scene shifts back to the public square.)

(This entire scene consists of the **HERALD** *and various* **ROYAL GUARDS** *trying to find the foot that fits the slipper. At first it may seem that the slipper is searching for the right foot, but with every* **WOMAN** *from six years old to ninety-three faced with the possibilities of marrying the* **PRINCE***, it is only a matter of time before a hundred feet are searching for the slipper. Perhaps a few* **GIRLS** *play a game of "keep-away" with the* **GUARDS** *after one gets ahold of the slipper. Perhaps a fight breaks out between an* **OLD LADY** *and a* **TEENAGER***. Perhaps a* **BEAUTY** *shows her leg, and the* **HERALD** *forgets what he's there for.)*

(Whatever the choreographer and the director work out, the "search" ends at Cinderella's house, which is moved into position as the public square is struck in the dark.)

Scene Four

(Cinderella's house. The **STEPMOTHER** *is seated,* **JOY** *and* **PORTIA** *stand behind her, and the* **HERALD** *is kneeling in front of the* **STEPMOTHER** *with the slipper. The* **STEPMOTHER** *is trying with great determination to squeeze her foot into the slipper. After a few grunts of pain, she gives up.)*

STEPMOTHER. It almost fits...does that count?

PORTIA. *(Snatching the slipper.)* Mother...honestly! It's my shoe. I'd know that shoe anywhere.

(The **STEPMOTHER** *reluctantly yields the chair to* **PORTIA,** *who sits and struggles with the slipper.)*

You see? It fits perfectly!

(She stands triumphantly and promptly falls on her face.)

JOY. *(Pulling the slipper off* **PORTIA***'s foot.)* Let me try! Let me try!

(She sits and tries to get the slipper to cooperate with her foot. When the **HERALD** *reaches to take the slipper back, she slaps his hand. The slipper simply won't fit on her foot, however.)*

(Turning to **PORTIA.***)*

What have you done to it? You've shrunk it!

(As she and **PORTIA** *join in an ad-lib argument, the* **HERALD** *neatly picks up the slipper.)*

HERALD. Is there anyone else in the house?

STEPMOTHER. No, there is nobody else here.

GODMOTHER. *(Appearing at the window.)* What about Cinderella?

STEPMOTHER. Nonsense!

HERALD. Who's Cinderella?

STEPMOTHER. Why, she's just a sort of chimney sweep and general helper here. There would be no use trying the slipper on her.

HERALD. We have instructions to try the slipper on everyone.

GODMOTHER. Try upstairs.

(The **HERALD** *and* **GUARDS** *go upstairs.)*

STEPMOTHER. *(To the* **GODMOTHER***.)* How dare you come poking your nose into my business?

GODMOTHER. I thought this was the prince's business. He is the one who is trying to find the missing girl, isn't he?

PORTIA. But Cinderella?

(She laughs her goofy laugh, and even **JOY** *looks almost amused.)*

GODMOTHER. Well, *she's* a girl.

HERALD. *(Returning.)* There's nobody up there.

GODMOTHER. *(Genuinely surprised.)* No one there?

STEPMOTHER. *(Triumphantly.)* I told you so.

(The **MEN** *troop out. The* **STEPMOTHER** *gloats at the* **GODMOTHER***, who looks very thoughtful.)*

PORTIA. Isn't that just like Cinderella? She hasn't even finished the laundry.

JOY. Or the floor.

PORTIA. And someone should really sweep out the fireplace...

(They begin to exit, continuing to list the things **CINDERELLA** *could be doing. The* **GODMOTHER** *crosses downstage, quite perplexed.)*

GODMOTHER. I don't understand... Cinderella not there... where could she be?

(Pause. Suddenly her face lights up.)

Of course! – I know...

(Blackout.)

[MUSIC NO. 32 "TRANSITION TO PALACE"]

*(The lights come up on the palace garden,
with the hedge units in.)*

Scene Five

*(**CINDERELLA** is discovered alone in the garden.
She sees someone coming from one side of the
stage and hides. The **PRINCE** enters and sits on
a bench. He looks most dejected. The **HERALD**
holds the cushion with the slipper.)*

PRINCE. ...And you tried the slipper on every young maiden?

HERALD. Every young maiden that could be found. I'm
sorry, Your Highness.

PRINCE. Mother was right. I'll never find her. Either she
doesn't exist or she's fled the kingdom. It is all a foolish
dream.

*(To the **HERALD**.)* Thank you. You may go.

*(The **PRINCE** bows his head more dejectedly
than before. The **HERALD** turns to leave but
pauses a moment, looking at the **PRINCE**. Very
quietly and with compassion, he places the
cushion with the slipper next to the **PRINCE** on
the bench. The **PRINCE** does not look up. The
HERALD motions with his head to the **GUARDS**,
and they exit silently.)*

*(The **PRINCE**, after a moment, looks over and
notices the slipper. He picks it up and studies
it. He starts to smile, but shakes it off. In a
gesture of utter defeat, he casually tosses the
slipper over his shoulder and into the bushes
up center. The **GODMOTHER** appears, catches
the slipper, and exits.)*

*(Believing everyone has gone, **CINDERELLA**
enters on the other side of the stage. She is
clearly very unhappy, and seems to be just
idly wandering, totally lost in thought, or
perhaps memory. She doesn't see the **PRINCE**
sitting on the bench. The **PRINCE** watches
her wander across the stage. His expression*

and his voice when he speaks are utterly
ingenuous.)

Who are you?

CINDERELLA. *(Startled and embarrassed.)* Oh... Oh! I'm
sorry. I didn't think... Excuse me, Your Highness, I had
no idea anyone was here... I'm sorry.

(Ashamed of her shabby dress and dirty face,
she quickly goes to leave.)

PRINCE. Wait!

*(***CINDERELLA** *freezes. He walks over to her.)*

You look familiar, somehow...at least I think you do
under all that grime. Do you work in the palace?

CINDERELLA. No, Your Highness.

PRINCE. I'm sure I've seen you before...or someone who
resembles you. Do you by any chance have a sister?

CINDERELLA. Two, Your Highness.

PRINCE. These sisters, were they at the ball?

CINDERELLA. Yes, Your Highness.

PRINCE. Do they look like you?

CINDERELLA. Well, they're stepsisters, Your Highness.

PRINCE. Stepsisters. Oh.

(He sits on the bench again, giving himself
up again to his sadness. **CINDERELLA** *looks*
around, uncertain of what to do. Her **PRINCE**
does not even remember her, and she herself
is uncertain whether she was really the girl
in last night's dream that the **PRINCE** *fell in*
love with. Perhaps she decides that she should
leave, but she finds she can't.)

CINDERELLA. Is there anything wrong, Your Highness?

PRINCE. Just the end of a dream. A dream that didn't come
true about a glass slipper that didn't fit anyone.

CINDERELLA. *(Coming closer to him.)* Oh, Your Highness,
you mustn't give up hope.

PRINCE. It was just a waste of time, a wild goose chase. It was impossible.

CINDERELLA. But, Your Highness, impossible things happen every day.

PRINCE. *(Skeptically.)* And even foolish dreams come true?

CINDERELLA. Oh, yes, Your Highness. If you wish hard enough and believe in what you're wishing, even foolish dreams come true.

> *(She has drawn closer and closer to the* PRINCE. *Now he looks at her very closely, as if for the first time.)*

PRINCE. Why do I feel...or am I just imagining... Who are you?

> *(CINDERELLA has moved down center, facing out.)*

CINDERELLA. *(Embarrassed.)* Oh...I'm just a girl from the village. I think I'd better go. My stepmother will be wondering where I am.

> *(She starts to leave.)*

PRINCE. *(Stopping her.)* Your stepmother wouldn't mind if you were a little late.

> *(He repeats the sentence to himself, trying to recall why it sounds so familiar.)*

...Wouldn't mind if you were a little late...

CINDERELLA. Really, Your Highness, I must go.

PRINCE. Yes, I suppose you must.

CINDERELLA. *(Backing away, reluctantly.)* Well. Goodbye, Your Highness.

PRINCE. Yes, goodbye.

> *(CINDERELLA moves farther away and begins to turn to go.)*

Wait!

> *(CINDERELLA hurries back toward him, but stops. She is confused and a little frightened.*

*She would blurt out all her feelings to him,
but she is afraid that perhaps it was a
dream and perhaps he would laugh at her.
Meanwhile, the* **GODMOTHER** *has entered up
center, unnoticed by the pair. In her hand is
the glass slipper the* **PRINCE** *had thrown away.
She sneaks over to the bench and replaces it
upon the cushion and exits unseen.)*

At least tell me your name.

CINDERELLA. Oh, it's a silly name. You wouldn't like it.

*(She hasn't heard anything that could
convince her she isn't making a fool of herself.
After telling the* **PRINCE** *to believe in his
dream, she is about to give up on her own.
She turns and begins to leave. The* **PRINCE**
*has turned and walked in the other direction,
back toward the bench, wrestling with the
familiarity of her words.)*

PRINCE. Silly name...wouldn't like it...

*(He suddenly sees the slipper back upon its
cushion. He seizes it up triumphantly.)*

Stop!

*(***CINDERELLA** *stops and turns around to face
him. He crosses slowly to her.)*

Did anyone try this slipper on you?

CINDERELLA. *(Uncertain how to answer.)* No...Your Highness.

(Slowly, the **PRINCE** *kneels in front of*
CINDERELLA, *removes her shoe, and places the
glass slipper on her foot. It fits perfectly.)*

PRINCE. *(Rising.)* I have found you. And I still do not know
your name.

CINDERELLA. My name is Cinderella.

PRINCE. The most beautiful name in the world.

[MUSIC NO. 33 "THE SLIPPER FITS"]

(The **PRINCE** *and* **CINDERELLA** *engage in the longest and most impassioned embrace yet. They kiss. They have found each other. Music segues to the wedding.)*

[MUSIC NO. 34 "FINALE: THE WEDDING"]

(In full view of the audience, the scene changes back to the ballroom for the Royal Wedding. The **COMPANY** *enters from both sides of the stage and helps prepare the scene for the wedding. The* **PRINCE** *and* **CINDERELLA** *are taken off to either side of the stage and, blocked by members of the* **COMPANY**, *are dressed for the wedding. The wedding processional begins when the preparations are complete. This is a grand and wonderful wedding, and everyone in the kingdom,* **JOY**, **PORTIA**, *and the* **STEPMOTHER** *included, has been invited.)*

(At the appropriate point in the music, the **PRINCE** *and* **CINDERELLA** *are standing in front of the* **MINISTER**. *The music stops as he says...)*

MINISTER. Dearly Beloved...

(And, appearing at the top of the stairs for her final godmotherly comment –)

GODMOTHER.
IMPOSSIBLE THINGS ARE HAPPENING EVERY DAY.
ENTIRE COMPANY.
DO I LOVE YOU
BECAUSE YOU'RE BEAUTIFUL?
OR ARE YOU BEAUTIFUL
BECAUSE I LOVE YOU?
AM I MAKING BELIEVE I SEE IN YOU
A GIRL TOO LOVELY TO
BE REALLY TRUE?
DO I WANT YOU
BECAUSE YOU'RE WONDERFUL?

OR ARE YOU WONDERFUL
BECAUSE I WANT YOU?
ARE YOU THE SWEET INVENTION OF A LOVER'S DREAM?
OR ARE YOU REALLY AS WONDERFUL AS YOU SEEM?

(Curtain.)

[MUSIC NO. 35 "BOWS"]

[MUSIC NO. 36 "EXIT MUSIC"]

The End